SWEEPING BEAUTIES

Rev. Cynthia T. Morse, OEF
4 Meeting House Hill Rd.
P.O. Box 179
Sanbornton, NH 03269-0179

Fairytales For Feminists

First published by
Attic Press,
44 East Essex Street,
Dublin 2.

Contrary fairies and other fairytales for feminists
    1. Short stories in English, 1945 — Special subjects: Feminism — Anthologies
    I. Crowley, Elaine   II. Kelly, Rita   III. Kelly, Maeve, *1930* —
    823'.01'08355 [FS]

ISBN 0-946211-71-X

2nd Ed. 1990

Illustrations: Barbara Nolan
Cover Design: Barbara Nolan
Typesetting: Phototype-Set Ltd., Dublin
Printing: The Guernsey Press

CONTENTS

'*Rapunzel's Revenge* is a feminist re-writing of fairy tales which has Mary Maher revealing that Snow White organised the seven dwarfs into a trade union; Maeve Binchy exposing Cinderella's prince as a foot fetishist; and a truly gifted Joni Crone showing that feminist fairy tales can be written in fairy tale language.' *In Dublin*

COVER DESIGN: Siobhan Condon
0 946211 18 3 £3.50

'*Ms Muffet* has transformed little Miss Muffet to Sturdy Ms Muffet who eats the spider, not her curds and whey. The Frog Prince is revisited by Princess Fergy who refuses to kiss him, but wants instead to add him to her frog collection.' *The Sunday Times*

COVER DESIGN: Wendy Shea
0 946211 27 2 £3.50

The third book in this successful series, *Mad And Bad Fairies* reveals Alice lost in Thunderland, a place inhabited by memblys and femblys; Ophelia's cunning plan of escape, and many more irreverent reinventions.

COVER DESIGN: Paula Nolan
0 946211 40 X £3.50

All: Fiction/Humour
150 x 120mm
Territory: W
Rights: Attic Press

The Fairy Godmother

ONCE upon a time there was a king who had a beautiful young daughter whose name was Phillipa. One morning the king sent for Phillipa and said, 'My dearest child, I have neglected you shamefully. Since your mother died you have been left to run wild. All that must now change.'

'But why, Papa?,' asked Phillipa smiling, fluttering her eyelashes and displaying her dimples, for she knew such things pleased her father.

'Because,' said the king, 'soon you must marry. And a man doesn't want a wild thing for a wife. No, indeed. A man wants a woman who will deport herself with decorum. A woman able to entertain his guests, rule his household and bear his children. A man likes his wife to look attractive, to be a credit to him, to be dignified, and above all else he wants her to be obedient — one who never, ever queries his decisions.'

'But aren't I decorous and obedient? Oh, sometimes I forget to brush my hair or pin it up if I've more important things on my mind. And sometimes I wear any old thing if it is comfortable. But I'm very good really.'

'Of course you are, but I'm a doting father and a lax one. A husband will expect a much higher standard.'

Phillipa pouted. 'I'm not sure I want a husband. It sounds a horrid idea.'

'Nonsense,' said her father. 'Women were made for marriage and besides I've lost my fortune — we are very poor. But you are very beautiful and I know just the prince for you.'

Phillipa wasn't at all keen at the prospect, but she loved her father dearly. Wanting to please him, she said 'Oh, very

6

well then, Papa.'

'Good girl,' her father said. 'I'll arrange a meeting in ten days' time. Let you and he get to know each other before any official announcement. Run along now, I've my accounts to look over.'

*   *   *   *

The king went to his counting house and counted out his money. There was less than he had thought. Time was pressing — he had better bring the meeting forward by one week. Phillipa went to the pantry and had some bread and honey — then into the garden to confide in the maid who was pegging out the clothes.

'Why are you complaining? Do you want to finish up an old maid like me, pegging out clothes for the rest of your life and forever tormented by blackbirds? Be grateful that a man will take and keep you.'

Disconsolately Phillipa went to find some friends and their sympathy.

'You lucky thing,' said the first one. 'I wish I had the chance of a husband.'

The second friend said, 'Think of all the beautiful gowns he will buy you. You'll be decked in diamonds for the rest of your life.'

The third one, whom Phillipa had always suspected of having a jealous nature, said, 'Grab the chance — after all you're not getting any younger. You are eighteen now, and the best marriages are made long before that.'

'Well, thanks very much — you were a great help,' said Phillipa to her friends and went off in a huff. But the two true friends followed her and talked and talked until they almost convinced her she was indeed a lucky girl.

*   *   *   *

All the same she had a little cry before she went to sleep

and wished for someone caring and wise to advise her. She slept and dreamed and into the dream came her Fairy Godmother. At first Phillipa didn't recognise her for she hadn't seen her since her christening.

'What's all this I hear about a wedding?,' asked the Fairy Godmother.

Putting on a brave face, Phillipa replied, 'Isn't it wonderful. I'm marrying a lovely prince and will live happily ever after.'

'Who says so?'

'Why, everybody — Papa, my friends, the maid.'

'Fiddlesticks! He wants you off his hands. The maid is demented, the blackbirds have scattered her wits — and as for those silly girls, what do they know about anything?'

'Oh, Fairy Godmother, don't be horrid.' Phillipa smiled and pouted and fluttered her lashes.

'And you can stop that for a start. The new women are learning not to depend on such ploys. I can see I've neglected you. That's what comes of having so many godchildren and having to spread the news. I'm absolutely exhausted — all this flying about.'

'You poor old thing,' said Phillipa. 'Do sit down, make yourself comfortable.'

The Fairy Godmother sat on the bed and yawned. 'Oh dear me,' she said, and yawned again. 'This will never do. Take hold of yourself. You've work to do. Where was I?'

'Saying fiddlesticks, that my friends are stupid and that you have to spread the news. What news?'

'Great news. Great news for women. We are beginning to throw off the shackles. That sort of thing.'

'But Fairy Godmother, only slaves are shackled.'

'Exactly. Slaves, that's what women have been. Bonded for life.'

'Surely not,' said Phillipa.

'Just think about it: first your father owns you, then your husband.'

'Yes. I see what you mean. Though I never thought of it

like that before. It sounds terribly exciting — do tell me more.'

'Well, first, there's to be no more matchmaking. A girl must have the right to choose her husband, or if she so wishes not choose one. But even more important, actually I think this should be first on the agenda, but there's a point of difference at conference level, a girl must be trained to earn her own living.'

'That's ridiculous. Princesses never work.'

'Ah, but supposing she won't always be a princess. Times are changing, many countries going for a republic. Kings and princes can be deposed, lose all their money. Like your father. Then what becomes of a princess?'

'Such a thought never crossed my mind.'

'Of course it didn't — that's why I'm here. In the olden days Fairy Godmothers bestowed gifts of beauty, patience, tolerance and forgiveness at christenings. All virtues to help a girl not go mad and kill herself or her husband after marriage. All that's changed. Do you know what gifts I bestow nowadays?'

'Tell me,' begged Phillipa.

'A true value on yourself, independence of spirit and, the important one, being able to earn your own living. Then after you've chosen your man, should he die, lose his fortune, or throw you out you'll be OK.'

'Okay? What a strange word, whatever does it mean?'

'That you'll be all right, I picked it up in America, you know that new place some Spaniard discovered. Lots of good ideas are coming out of America, especially for women.'

'I like the new ideas, I really like them,' said Phillipa, bouncing in the bed with excitement. 'This economic independence — how does one go about it?'

'You have to train for a trade or a profession. A girl of your class could be a Fairy Godmother. The course is great fun and nowadays you get a salary.'

'I see,' said Phillipa thoughtfully, and was silent for a

while. Then she said, 'Yes, I'd like that, but I still want to marry.'

'Well, of course. But now it would be your choice and with an equal partnership. Everything shared, money, decisions, everything.'

'But what about Papa?'

'That's where you test your mettle. Because it's your first test, I'll be hovering near in case you falter. Goodnight now and sweet dreams.'

*   *   *   *

The next morning at breakfast Philippa took a deep breath and said, 'Papa, I am not going to marry the Prince.'

The King choked on his toast. When he had finished coughing and spluttering he said, 'You'll do as I say.' His voice was loud and angry.

Phillipa's decision wavered. 'But Papa,' she said falteringly. Then she heard the voice of her Fairy Godmother: 'I'm right behind you. Stand your ground and no simpering, no pleading.'

Phillipa took another deep breath. 'I'm quite serious, Papa. Times are changing. Women are no longer chattels. Before I marry I want to have a profession, a trade.'

'You want to be like a man,' barked her father.

'Oh no, I love being a woman — but not a slave.'

What is the world coming to? the king thought. Then suddenly he remembered something his soothsayer had told him recently. 'Strange times are coming. Women in the land will revolt. But it will pass. While it lasts humour them.' So, said the king to himself, the strange times have arrived. And humour my darling daughter I will. I can borrow against my crown until she comes to her senses. The prince is a good fellow, he'll understand.

'Perhaps,' said the king, and his smile was benign, 'I was hasty. Forgive me, my dear child, and tell me again, what brought about this change of heart?'

Philippa told him. 'I see,' said the king, and stroked his beard. 'Tell me darling child, this independence, this career — what did you have in mind?'

'I'd like to be a Fairy Godmother.'

The king could scarcely conceal his amusement. A Fairy Godmother! Harmless creatures who twittered about cradles bestowing their gifts. Phillipa would soon tire of that. He really must tell his soothsayer — how he would laugh. He composed his expression and spoke with great seriousness. 'I suppose one must move with the times, and if that is your choice of a career I won't raise any objection.'

'Thank you, Papa, oh thank you,' said Phillipa and was about to be more effusive when she remembered her new status.

The king nodded his acceptance while keeping a straight face. And round and round the room flew the Fairy Godmother chortling with glee.

Elaine Crowley

Revenge Of The Sisters Grimm

This is a tale of the Sisters Grimm
who lived in the land of he and him
a culture formed by class and clan
a society tailor-made for man.
The laws of former Patri-Ark
Kept sisters past hid in the dark,
where rules were made by he for she
and written out of his story.
No trace was found of woman-kind
save what the bravest one could find
by delving through the olden lore
of memory, songs and tales of yore.

ÖNCE upon a time — not old god's time, since no one remembers her — rather, once upon another time there were three sisters Grimm. They lived in the land of society, and they had reason aplenty for feeling grim. You see, our sisters suspected that they'd been 'suckered' by society. They were only recently aware that society had spent many happy years playing 'Gotcha' with them and all their sisters. Society at that time was a state or place of perfect happiness ... if you were a man. Man made all the rules in his own image ... and interests.

In order to understand and change this phenomenon, the Sisters Grimm founded the nons' collective. They wished to arrive at a new understanding of society and how it works, or rather society and how it makes women work. The first nons' discussion centred round the origins of 'Gotcha'. The Elder Sister Grimm — who was gifted with insight — said she believed that 'Gotcha' happened at the very moment a female child was born. 'This wasn't always so,' she said. Her insight told her about a time in the past when women ruled their own lives.

The sisters grimly agreed to trace their roots to prove the Elder Grimm right. They marched to the Hall of Patriarkives and began the long search back. They were astonished to find absolutely no trace or trail of womankind. 'How can this be,' cried the Sisters Grimm, 'surely our sisters past made some mark upon society?' But alas, No! The arkives contained only his story. The annals were full of He and Him. Sisters, wives, mothers and daughters were not worthy of record. 'I know,' said the middle Sister Grimm — who was gifted with vision, 'we must look for the secret sign.'

'What is the secret sign?' said the younger sister Grimm.

'The secret sign of our sisters past is made known only to the "special ones". We must look for it in all the secret places of woe-man-woe.'

And sure enough, our sisters were lucky enough or special enough to find the secret mark. They spent many months unravelling the source of her story. They unearthed old maps and stories and came upon the Myth of the Matri-arks. This was a legend whose truth was shrouded by the mists of time. But their instincts made them pursue the story. And by following all the signs and symbols found on castles, keeps and mounds, they uncovered the origins of the Matri-arks.

The Grimms found their new task very healing. They learned about a time and place where woman ruled in harmony with nature. All the natural laws were strictly observed. In fact, nature was their religion. They took nothing from the earth without giving something in return. Their laws were based on love, justice and respect for all and violence was alien to their lives. All was not good, however. A certain breed of man was not content with peace and harmony. These men, known ever after as Patri-arks, wanted to upset this natural order. They plotted, planned and consulted with evil logics to draw up a plan and gain supremacy. This mighty plan contained the seeds of today's society. They developed a plan of class and clan where women did the real work and men met in small groups to discuss science, maths and other concepts, thereby increasing their store of knowledge.

And so, time came to pass and men came to power. They had control over our sisters who slowly but ever gradually lost all their skills. They allowed the secrets of the earth, sky and sea to lapse in their memory. The store of lore about animals, herbs and plants was eroded from their minds. All the old customs fell by the wayside. They no longer passed on the knowledge from mother to daughter at puberty. The onset of menses, known as 'the special sign' was no longer a joyous celebration. Instead, it became a hidden secret discussed only by women.

The Grimms returned to society armed with their fury plus the new information about the old ways and secrets. They ran feminars and consciousness-raising sessions and became the leaders of a quiet revolution. Slowly but surely sisters of many lands became initiated into the new order. By using wiles and guiles they insinuated themselves into positions of power, influence. In time men came to depend on them totally. All that remained was the Grimm revenge.

And it came to pass that the male cabinet wished to host an intersocietal debate. They sensed the winds of change and wished to reassert their power. The cabinet consulted with the image-makers — who were the sisters in disguise. And the Grimms sold them the notion of wearing the new light-weight suits of psychic energy.

'They will cover you with a powerful aura,' said the younger sister Grimm. She explained about the psychic suits being at an experimental stage.

'Are you willing to use them?'

'Yes, yes,' said the greedy cabinet members.

'Order them now.'

The big night dawned. The TV cameras stood by to

witness the debate. There was to be satellite coverage of the most important event of the year. In marched the powerful and pompous. They stood before the cameras poised and perspiring.

'Right,' said the Elder Grimm, 'SHOOT!'

Out popped the Middle Grimm. She aimed the laser-beam at the entire host of Patri-arks. And their wonderful suits of psychic energy disintegrated before the entire land.

'Bald exposure of the men and all their peccadillos!'

'How the mighty are fallen,' grinned the Grimms as the entire nation convulsed at the sight of the greatest 'gotcha' of all time.

Cathleen O'Neill

Pygmalion

T HE location is London, the weather is foggy. It is the time of detective stories. Emily Johnson struggles on and off buses clutching that magical thing, a publisher's contract.

After a long period of dreaming about being a famous writer and a longer period of having her work rejected by every conceivable publisher, Emily's stories had finally found their way into print. Not into the kind of print Emily had anticipated. In her dreams she had become a frequent contributor to the literary journals she admired (but never read through). In her dreams she had become the 'major new talent' of a major old publishing house. In fact she became this year's or this month's or this week's new 'queen of crime'. Her stories appeared in magazines where young women with astonishing cleavages fell across the cover without a tremor of platinum blonde or a smudge of lipstick.

Rita's first collection of stories has just been accepted by Clarke, Carson and Clarke, a very new firm of minor publishers who had offered Emily the unbelievable sum of five hundred pounds in advance royalties. Before she reaches her shabby bed-sit that evening Emily decides to move out of it. She would find a service flat perhaps (no, five hundred wouldn't keep that up for long). Two or three rooms overlooking the river would be nice, something 'simple and elegant' and rather like the flat she had invented for Rowenna Pringle.

Rowenna featured in half a dozen of the stories which Clarke, Carson and Clarke had decided to publish. They had been delighted to hear that Emily planned to develop a full-length novel around this heroic and beautiful female detective.

Clarke, Carson and Clarke were of the opinion that there was an avid public demand for just such an innovation in crime fiction as a female ex-police inspector, aged 26, with a black-belt in karate. 'Changing times, you know, changing times.' Clarke, Carson and Clarke had given a most disagreeable wink.

Rowenna was going to make Emily's fortune. In the first story featuring her female detective Emily had named her Letitia. Trying to imagine how early one might expect to retire from the police force with the rank of inspector and calculating it would take a woman a few years longer than a man, Emily had initially described Miss Pringle as a stout 54-year-old in tweeds. The editors of *Detective Omnibus* had detected that its avid public was not quite ready for a middle-aged heroine who packed a tough punch. In the interests of the ten pounds on offer if she did so, Emily made a few changes. Rowenna was born, and Emily paid her most pressing debts.

The income from the stories brightened Emily's life considerably. She even contemplated giving up her job as secretary to the London Paintmakers' Guild and writing full-time. Such heady aspirations had so far been undermined by Emily's propensity for rapid spending of her 'story money', as she called it. First her down-at-heel, largely second-hand book collection was aggrandised. Her name disappeared from the reserve lists of public libraries and shiny new hard-covers appeared on her shelves. As demand and payment for the stories increased, new shelves were required. Emily acquired a tailored suit — necessary, she thought, for meetings with publishers. As she worked all day and wrote stories most of the night, Emily's prosperity manifested itself mostly in the purchase of small domestic luxuries; books, chocolates, silk stockings, brandy, new clothes she never wore, and two expensive modern art prints which looked so startling against the bed-sit's floral wallpaper that she put them under the bed. These little vanities were reflected, magnified, in the tales. Rowenna

Pringle wore profusions of silk, her tailored suits came from the best designers and she quoted contemporary literature sadly at the end of each case.

Rowenna's cases were always murders. She considered anything less a waste of her talents and had parted company with the police force when it had tried to confine her to a desk in the fraud investigations division. Emily was universally acclaimed as delightfully ingenious in her execution of murders for Rowenna to solve. The first of Rowenna's cases had concerned the apparently random killing of young women. The police believed that the women, whom they found difficult to identify, were chance victims of a maniac. Rowenna, by processes entirely incomprehensible to the police, proved the murders to have been the carefully planned work of a secret, criminal society, executed for complex, particular and pecuniary motives.

Most of the murder victims in Emily's stories were women, until *Detective Omnibus* asked her for a story set in aristocratic circles, preferably located in what they described as a 'gentle nook of rural England'. So Emily mysteriously murdered Lord So-and-So and Rowenna discovered the murder to have been carried out by a young woman whose sister had died in an industrial accident in one of the aforementioned Lord's factories. Emily entered into a long correspondence with *Detective Omnibus* about the propriety of her ending: Rowenna had arrived at Southampton just as the avenging sister had set sail for South America. The usually moralistic detective had not only failed: she had remarked that this failure was a relief to her. (Rowenna had never before failed to apprehend anyone.) *Detective Omnibus* were of the opinion that such sympathy for a murderess was liable to disturb the moral sensibilities of their readers — *Detective Omnibus* was always adamant that its trade in crime was undertaken to profit morality. Emily, in the *Omnibus'* opinion, had better stick to killing off shop-girls and Rowenna should know better.

Despite its moral defects, 'Murder at the Manor' had had

some selling points. An entertaining young person by the name of Peter Dashiell had appeared in it. He was the deceased's nephew, heir to his vast fortune and the primary police suspect in the case. Having given him the fourth degree, knocked him out by accident in the dark and saved him from the gallows, Rowenna had persuaded this gentleman to improve safety conditions in the factories he inherited. (Emily still harbours a grievance against the *Omnibus* on this issue. The long dialogue on industrial safety codes and practices which she had painstakingly researched was excised from the printed story.)

. Peter Dashiell would make an excellent detective, thought the *Omnibus*, who were possibly not so in tune with the time as Clarke, Carson and Clarke. Could Dashiell perhaps rescue Rowenna Pringle in a subsequent adventure? This suggestion so outraged Emily that she and her female detective left the *Omnibus* out of temper with the editors and their hero and considerably out of pocket.

So Emily stayed with the London Paintmakers' Guild. As we rejoin her on her way home with her precious contract, she suffers a moment of misgiving. Writer now writes and detective now detects exclusively for Carson, Clarke and Carson.

She shakes off her anxiety as she lights the fire in her room. She must concentrate on the plot of this present novel — the contract specifies quite definite dates for the submission of her forthcoming books.

Emily beats eggs abstractedly. She has been speculating for weeks on a variety of murderous plots. (She currently favours death of a marine biologist in a sealed compression tank.) Her unwillingness to choose irrevocably any one of these has ensured that only three hundred words of the Rowenna novel have found their way to paper. As she pours the eggs on to the pan she thinks she should read this brave 300 through — again.

She once again reaches the point where Rowenna has settled down to unwind after a case with a glass of fine brandy and a leather-bound first edition. Then Emily's eggs burn and she is scraping the edible parts out of the pan when she remembers Peter Dashiell. She had thought of developing the character in successive Rowenna Pringle stories before those fool editors had taken him up as a cause. He had been rather engaging and innocent before he got mixed up with editors.

The eggs are vile. Emily pours herself a drink to celebrate the contract, nibbles a little cheese and toast and sits down at her typewriter. A clause or two, and she has settled Rowenna a little more comfortably in her armchair. What to do now? Emily adjusts the ribbon, gets up, draws the curtains and puts coal on the fire. She might bring Dashiell in for light relief just after the second or third murder. (Emily is a novice, but even a novice queen of crime does not expect to sustain three hundred pages on one little murder.)

Back at the typewriter she sips a little brandy. Here goes, she thinks. Rowenna got up from her chair, suddenly restless. Mist crept up to the window and the sight of it sent a chill through her despite the heat of her room. She drew the curtains against the deserted street and put a little coal on the fire. She thought she heard something in the hall, the cat perhaps, listened a moment, still and intent, but outside there was only silence. Rowenna thought this last case must have disturbed her. Though it had been mundane, it had been brutal. A holiday would be nice, she thought, as she settled back in the chair and stretched her feet to the fire. Paris perhaps. Rowenna slowly dozed off.

This is hopeless, thinks Emily. Vague noises in the hallway! I have to come up with a little action soon. Someone will creep up on her as she sleeps. But who?

The first thing Rowenna was aware of when she woke was the swish of the door over the carpet. The man closed it behind him. He was well-dressed. A long trench coat with a turned-up collar made it difficult to discern more without fully opening her eyes. She stayed very still until he had almost reached her. Then she sprang. He fell silently. He was lying face down on the floor with her knee in the small of his back before he even had a chance to gasp.

'Not a professional anyway', said Rowenna as she secured his feet and hands with his long scarf. 'Now let's see who we have.' She rolled him over with her foot.

Now let's see how the editors like this, thinks Emily, no longer distinguishing between progressives and conservatives, clarkes and omnibuses.

'Peter', exclaimed Rowenna.

'Let me up, for heaven's sake. What do you think you're doing anyway, jumping on people like that! You didn't even give me a second to explain.'

'Explain now, then. What are you doing breaking in here and creeping up on me like that?'

The indignant gentleman writhed in considerable discomfort. He rightly judged Rowenna's curiosity to be more powerful than her caution and refused to answer any questions until released. He then installed himself in her chair by the fire.

Emily pauses. Is it really a good idea to resurrect Peter Dashiell after all the trouble he caused last time? Well, it's either that or back to vaguenesses in the hall.

Rowenna poured herself a drink to replace the one overturned in her tussle with her visitor. His eyes followed the bottle. She pointedly did not offer him one. (Emily is still a little out of temper with this pretender to Rowenna's status as detective.)

'I'm waiting,' Rowenna said.

'I'm afraid,' said Peter, 'I'm in a spot of bother again.'

'Don't tell me you've inherited another fortune.'

'There is no need to be sarcastic. Just listen for a while. The police may catch up with me here any minute.'

'If you think I'm going to allow you to be arrested on my premises . . .' Rowenna's voice was still irritated but her face was beginning to register interest. 'What have you done?'

'I did not do it,' Dashiell's self-importance was fast fading into panic. 'Please, Rowenna. You're the only detective I know — apart from the divorce chaps. You have to help me.'

Rowenna poured him a drink.

'Now,' she said, 'tell me.'

It was all very simple really. (Emily here briefly contemplates introducing the tale of the marine biologist, decides against it and commences to improvise.) Peter Dashiell had been spending a quiet week-end in the country with about two dozen friends, doing a little fishing and a lot of nothing much. He, a young woman named Natalie Fisher and two other couples had gone hill-walking. That is to say the party had driven five miles to a hill, walked two miles up it, declared itself parched, opened bottles and had a picnic. Some two hours later, Peter Dashiell and Natalie Fisher had decided to venture a little further in search of a particularly scenic view they had heard about. The rest of the party declined to join them. About 40 minutes later Peter returned alone, saying he and Natalie had quarrelled about which direction to take back and that she would no doubt find her way back shortly. She did not. An hour went by, then two. It grew dark. At first the party was merely irritated at being kept waiting, then it became anxious. They began to search for the missing woman, but their search was impeded by darkness and by the quantity of alcohol consumed in the afternoon. Finally one of the women took a car and went to the nearest village for help. By the time the police arrived the other members of the party were sober and distressed. Peter was blaming himself for having left her.

The police found the body within an hour of their arrival. It was under some bushes at the muddy edge of the small lake she and Peter had gone to see. Natalie Fisher had been stabbed three times in the chest with a small hunting-knife she had worn in her belt for effect. Her companions were shocked. The police thought it just what might be expected among that fast crowd. Still, they were sorry for the girl. And one of them would have to go to the door of a house somewhere and tell her family.

One curious fact about the case did please the police. The muddy ground around the body yielded very distinct footprints. Just two sets. One was Natalie's. The other — the alacrity of the police in discovering this had been impressive — was that of Peter Dashiell.

Dashiell looked poised to burst into another assertion of innocence, so Rowenna took control of the narrative.

'Time of death?' she enquired brusquely.

'That's just it,' Peter Dashiell replied. 'It can't have been long after I left her.'

'Any motive on your part?'

Here Dashiell faltered.

'No, there isn't, not really . . .'

'But the police think there is?'

'Well, actually we had rather a row the evening before . . . before *it* happened.'

'And it was overheard?'

Dashiell nodded. He was seized by dread at the prospect of revealing the source of the quarrel.

'I'd rather not say what it was about.'

'And I would rather not have clients who are not entirely honest and open with me!' Rowenna was really angry, but Dashiell was not to be swayed. The argument deteriorated into sullen silence on both sides, with Dashiell staring into the fire in a melancholy fashion while Rowenna glared at him. She roused herself, and was about to order him out of the house when she realised he had fallen asleep in the chair. He certainly didn't look like a murderer, sitting there in that chair, his head to one side. He was rather handsome, though his mannerisms tended to obscure his attractions when he was awake. Asleep, he looked fair, young and generally adapted to be charming . . .

Emily is at once restless and sleepy. She stretches, once then twice, feeling the strain of typing ebb out of her back. I need coffee, she thinks, but she only moves to the armchair by the fire. She stretches her feet towards the heat. Then she dozes and she dreams.

The first thing Emily is aware of when she wakes is the swish of the door over the carpet. She jumps from her chair with a start and reaches for the poker.

'Put that down, silly girl.' The woman who addresses Emily is wiry, middle-aged and very authoritative.

'What do you want?' Emily tries to imitate the cool tone she attributes to her detective, but her voice sounds cracked and nervous.

'I want to give you a little advice. Before you do something very foolish. You are under no circumstances to fall in love with that young man.'

'What young man?'

'Peter Dashiell, of course.'

Emily relaxes. She understands fully. She is still asleep. She sits back in the chair and closes her eyes.

'Don't shut your eyes when I'm speaking to you.'

Emily opens just one eye and squints at this extraordinary intruder. The woman looks familiar, though Emily is sure she has never met her before. She might be an older relative of someone Emily knows.

'I cannot believe you do not recognise me,' says the intruder, as if reading Emily's thoughts. 'I am Rowenna Pringle.'

Emily reaches for the poker again, but Miss Pringle kicks it out of her grasp with surprising dexterity. Emily has read about lunatics who think they are Napoleon or Elizabeth the First. She is pondering whether they might be a dangerous breed when the intruder startles her again.

'I suppose you think I don't know what you're up to with this novel of yours? It is really quite bad enough you dressing me in the most unsuitable clothing for detective work and having me spout poetry in that ridiculous way. I understand you have to make a living and so on.'

Emily blinks, pinches herself and reaches for the brandy.

'You don't have to take to drink over it.' The older woman grins for a minute. 'You stood up to those *Detective Omnibus* people splendidly. Couldn't have done better myself.'

'Yourself?'

'Myself. Inspector Rowenna Pringle, retired. Rowenna is all wrong, you know,' Miss Pringle has the air of a kindly schoolteacher correcting spellings. 'Mother and Father were much too sensible to call one Rowenna.'

Emily is on her second brandy. Perhaps that is why she begins to feel more at ease with the situation. Best to play along with the bewildered old woman.

'And why are you here tonight, Miss Pringle?' she asks.

'Why am I here? Because you want me to help a murderer go free, that's why I'm here tonight. "Fair and young and generally adapted to be charming" my hat. Murderers are always charming. Don't you ever read those magazines you write for?'

Emily's head is reeling. No-one has read those pages but herself. She saw the woman come through the door, she didn't have any chance to read the page sitting upright in the typewriter.

'Are you really ... I mean you can't be, can you?' she stutters.

'Now don't waste my time disbelieving me. You just listen. That Dashiell fellow killed that girl as certainly as I'm standing here before you.' Emily thinks she sees a shadow of a smile on her visitor's face at this point.

Miss Pringle continues. 'He is going to say that he won't reveal the source of the quarrel because he wants to protect the dead girl's reputation.'

'That had occurred to me,' says Emily.

'Had it now? And I suppose it had occurred to you that I was going to fall in love with him for his sweet, honourable nature and rescue him from the gallows just in time?'

Looking at Miss Pringle, such a development seems suddenly inappropriate to Emily.

'Well, I didn't think of you quite as you are, you know.'

'You did originally. You were corrupted by the measly sum of ten pounds, as I recall. *Don't* tell me about your rent arrears, I *don't* want to know.'

Emily cannot decide whether to be ashamed or frightened by this display of insight into her affairs. There is no reasonable explanation for this bizarre situation, so she must take it on its own terms.

'How do you know he did it?' she asks.

'That, of course, is your immediate concern. No doubt you will argue his innocence to me,' Miss Pringle is most contemptuous. 'It is perfectly simple really. The crime was not premeditated. They went up there together to talk things over. She had discovered some secret of his, something to do with sex or drugs, I can't tell which. Do you know yet?'

'I don't know any of this,' says Emily, 'and if you are a character in my story I don't see how you can know more than I do. I certainly don't see how you can know the story before I've written it.'

'I'm guessing a lot, but you gave me this wonderful and infallible deductive process. I'm infallibly deducing that that chap I left asleep in my rooms is guilty.' Miss Pringle is a more dogmatic woman than Rowenna used to be. 'You had me say in "The Little House Murder" that the obvious is always true, but it is often difficult to see the obvious. Dreadful trite things you have me say at times. Anyway, in this case it is true. Two sets of footprints went in. One set came out. Therefore the owner of the set that came out killed the owner of the set that stayed in. Simple. He will have left swimming stuff on the far side of the lake by now, I suppose, knowing I'll find them. The lake is too shallow and full of reeds for that, of course. Any swimmer would become entangled in the reeds and drown. One might wade across, but there would be traces of that.'

'If he did it, then why did he come to you, the infallible detective?' asks Emily, who is very annoyed at this dismissal of her next projected turn in the plot.

'He underestimates me, my dear girl. Which is not surprising considering how much you've watered me down these past few months. He wants me to find out the exact time of death for him. He has an alibi constructed with one of those inane friends of his, but he can't use it until I prove she died later than the police think at present. He knows she died later of course, because he killed her. I must say, it will be quite an ingenious story if you do it right. The readers will think he must be innocent, since he is my client, and then at the end, after many twists and turns to confuse them, he will be revealed as the villain. Very neat. Though you will of course ruin it if you have me ogling him so. It is really much too common for detectives to send their loved ones to jail.'

'Surely he'll be hanged?' Emily's voice is really very melancholy.

'Manslaughter,' says Miss Pringle.

'No,' says Emily. 'I won't do it. I wouldn't turn him into a detective for *Detective Omnibus* and I won't turn him into a murderer for you.'

'If you are going to write detective stories you had better learn to think of the consequences. What will happen if you let this fellow go? You know perfectly well it will be much the better story if he did it. You know that is the right way to end it. And what about me? If I connive in letting a villain go free my reputation will be ruined. Worse, you will have people think I fell in love with that vacuous creature. You will become a sentimental novelist. Either that or you'll end up writing those psychological studies the critics love. You know, the ones where you see everything from the murderer's point of view and it's really his poor wife's fault he put weedkiller in her tea.' Miss Pringle's indignation is perfectly ferocious. 'Well? Is that what you want?'

Emily did think initially that Peter Dashiell should be a villain this time, but then she had made him so very handsome and charming.

'I'll do it your way,' she tells Miss Pringle, but when she turns towards Miss Pringle the infallible detective has disappeared.

*　　*　　*　　*

Next morning Emily reads through the story she completed in the night. Peter Dashiell was anything but charming when they dragged him off to jail. She puts it away in a drawer and turns her mind to the marine biologist in the compression chamber. 'I wonder,' she thinks, 'what Miss Pringle will make of this. She may even come and tell me.' On the whole Emily rather hopes that she will.

Gerardine Meaney

Alice In Thunderland

Prologue

In *Ms Muffet & Mad and Bad Fairies* we learned how Alice had drifted onto the shore of Thunderland, a strange place with strange customs. For instance a fem or fembly was a female person who might only speak during chatter time. Alice narrowly escaped a peculiar but dangerous attack when it was discovered she spoke for herself. In the last chapter she actually encountered a fembly and with her landed in the Funnery from which she and the fembly are just now escaping.

Now read on for more exciting adventures.

Chapter Three

LICE and the fembly reached the sunflower mouth just as the petals were closing inwards. 'Hurry, hurry,' gasped the fembly. 'If the flower closes on us we will never get out. We will be stuck here in the Funnery for ever and ever.'

A fate to be avoided, Alice realised, grasping the fembly by the hair and swimming strongly towards the exit. Behind them the funns called, 'Wait, wait dear sisters. Wait for our reunion. We will have a lovely get-together if you only wait.'

'They want to eat us,' the fembly gurgled through mouthfuls of water. 'I just know they want to eat us. They will eat us up and spit us out when they have finished.'

Alice was too busy swimming to reply. She had to push her way very strongly through the sunflower petals, which were sticky and clingy and heavily scented. In fact, the perfume was so strong it made Alice almost sleepy and when she looked down at the fembly she realised that her new friend was indeed fast asleep.

'An interesting attempt at control,' Alice mused. Then they were out through the opening and into the undergrowth and suddenly her feet touched the ground. In the distance she saw a chink of blue light which she realised was the tunnel down which they had tumbled. The fembly was by now snoring her head off so Alice tucked her under her arm and made for the opening. Rocks, rubble and clay were piled up in an irregular pyramid and Alice clawed her way up it. About twenty feet separated her from the chink of blue light. She uncoiled her whip from around her waist and whirled it around her head, carefully aiming at the exit. In a single throw it was hooked into the earth above and she swung herself and her friend up its length and out into the open again.

The fembly woke up just as they flopped onto the ground.

'Wha' ... wha' happened?' she asked. She didn't wait for an answer but proceeded with the next question. 'Did we miss the happening?'

'I don't know about that,' Alice said. 'But we missed being caught in the sunflower palace with the funns. A pretty difficult place to escape from, by the look of it.'

'It is, it is,' the fembly agreed. 'You have to get a pupil dissipation. And you might never get it. You have to apply in hectiplate and wait for a millennium of years which may or may not come. But you might like it there. Some people do.'

'You told me the funns were banished years ago because they were too powerful. You also said that all the singing and laughing and making and doing goes on there. Why would anyone want to stay in a place of banishment? I do not think I would like to be banished,' said Alice. 'And I don't think I would like to have to sing and laugh and make and do. I might like to think. I might like to cry. I might like to be sad.'

'You are not allowed to be sad,' the fembly said miserably.

'When femblies are sad we cry too much and we make enormous rivers. We create confusion, you know. When there's trouble, sachet la fembly.'

'What does that mean?' Alice asked with interest.

'I don't know,' the fembly said. 'How would I know? I'm just told and I believe what I am told. Faith is the thing. We must have faith.'

'Faith in what?' Alice asked for the sake of politeness, although she was beginning to find the conversation a little dull. She was a strange creature, this fembly, and yet it was hard not to like her. She had an amusing turn of phrase, thought Alice.

'Just faith. We'd better watch it. We are beginning to ask too many questions. I think I asked two questions a while ago. That could be my quota.' She began to count nervously on her fingers.

Fancy having a quota of questions, thought Alice. There were many irritating aspects to this Thunderland and she was beginning to wish she had never drifted onto its shore. The very first opportunity she got she would leave it. She looked down at the fembly trotting along beside her and she wondered what would happen to her when she left her.

'Are you going to meet the membly you left fishing?'

'Oh no,' replied the fembly. 'He'll have found a new fembly for himself. Someone prettier and more glamorous than me. I was only a trial. I was his practice. I am always the practice.'

'What did you practise?' asked Alice.

'The usual things,' the fembly said. 'Slaving and choring and hearing and hooring.'

'It sounds disgusting,' Alice said.

'You get used to it,' the fembly replied philosophically. 'It's bad in the beginning because everything is all mixed up and you don't know which thing you are supposed to be doing. Sometimes you do the hooring and then you discover you should have been doing the choring and sometimes you do the hearing and then you realise you should have been doing the slaving. But after a while you begin to get the hang of it. The trouble is that when you're a practice you've just managed to understand the membly you have got and you're finished with him and you have to go to another one. Memblies use up a lot of femblies.'

'And were you always a practice or did you become one?' Alice asked.

'I became one, of course.' The fembly seemed annoyed by Alice's question. 'You think I always looked like this. I was once pretty, you know.'

'I think you're pretty now,' Alice said politely. She had no idea what it meant, but she could see that it was important to the fembly.

'It doesn't matter if *you* think I am pretty,' the fembly said rudely. 'It's what the others think that matters.'

'The memblies?'

'Yes and no. They make some of the prettiness rules. But it is the OTHERS who make the most rules. I can't explain it, and if you keep asking any more questions someone is bound to pick them up on the wavelengths and you will be tied to a stake and burned and you wouldn't like that, I can tell you.'

Alice burst out laughing. 'I'd like to see them try,' she said. 'Tie me to a stake! Burn me! What a joke.'

She was sorry she laughed because the fembly clapped her little hands to her pointy little ears and began to rock to and fro.

'Hale and rainbow, all hale and stones, pallyoola, afem. afem. so be it,' she chanted and began to bob up and down, tipping her knee to the ground and then bowing her forehead until it touched the ground.

'You want to be careful,' Alice said. 'That is muddy.'

'She knoweth not what she sayeth,' the fembly cried. 'She knoweth not what she doeth.'

'I certainly do know what I sayeth and I certainly do know what I doeth,' Alice protested. But the poor fembly had such a look of anguish on her face and she was so busy contorting herself into the oddest positions that Alice knew she was truly upset. And it occurred to Alice then that she had shut off all her own insights and instincts since she had come to this strange place and that she was beginning to lose the powers of understanding and of feeling.

'I am very sorry,' she said. 'I am very, very sorry. I apologise.'

'Oh, thank goodness,' the fembly straightened up. 'I thought you would never say it. You're some dumb broad, believe me.'

'I believe you,' Alice said sincerely. To her amazement the fembly smiled, a funny lop-sided quiver of a smile but still a smile.

They had come to a cross-road of a sort.

'This is the Hand,' the fembly said. 'The thumb is the short road to Wordy which is where all the fine talkers live. You need a pass for it and I don't have one. The forefinger goes to the Safe Confinement, the middle finger goes to the Boxing Match, the fourth finger —'

'I would like to see the Boxing Match,' Alice interrupted, her enthusiasm getting the better of her politeness. 'Do they box matches or match boxes?'

'You get weirder by the minute,' said the fembly. 'I have a feeling you won't like this.' The moment she said the words she clapped her hand over her mouth in horror and then to Alice's amazement she pulled her oddly shaped striped skirt over her face and began to rock to and fro. At the same time a siren screeched around them and a loud voice began to hector and command.

'Who is it that cometh over the mountain? Who is it that hath a feeling? Who is it that useth the word like? Likes and dislikes, feelings and emotions. The fembly diseases have almost been conquered, the virus of feeling almost destroyed. Who would run the risk of its renewal? Speak up. Identify yourself. Confess your sin and do penance.'

'I confess to all right and wrong. I confess to blather, jung and holy fraud,' the fembly gabbled, frantically turning around in circles as she did so, 'that I have sinned impedingly, and withered the power of seed. My own fault, my own fault, my own fault. I'm to blame I'm to blame I'm to blame. I did it I did it I did it. I said it I said it I said it. Sachet la fembly, sachet la fembly.'

Alice looked everywhere for the source of the voice and just as the fembly had finished her frantic gyrations she noticed a familiar object on top of a nearby tree. Pulling out her whip, she flicked it in that direction. There was a splutter of blue and the object came tumbling down. It crackled for a few seconds and then went dead.

'A primitive piece of equipment,' Alice remarked, examining it. 'A microphone picks up the vibration, probably tuned to particular words, and then the loudspeaker broadcasts the recorded message. Why did it frighten you?'

But the fembly had run off across the fields, wobbling from side to side, her skirt pulled up over her eyes, her spiky heels almost tripping her. Alice sighed pityingly and continued on her journey.

About an hour later (as measured by Harmony time which was the only time she knew) Alice arrived at a clearing. Gathered in a circle was a large group of memblies dressed in splendid robes of purple and gold and wearing exotic head dresses shaped like pyramids, embroidered with gold and silver thread with insets of rubies and emeralds. Other memblies wore black jerkins over black tights which showed off their knees and calves to great effect. There was much hammering and sawing and Alice saw that a platform was being erected. Two femblies sat with the memblies. They were clad in grey from head to toe in a sort of wraparound garment from which only their eyes were seen.

Alice sat where she could not be seen and reflected on her adventures to date. She closed her eyes and dozed for a while.

She was wakened by the sounding of a brass gong.

'Bedoing, bedoing', it went booming through the clearing and echoing off the nearby woodland. One of the memblies climbed onto the platform which was now ringed by ropes and called in an important voice: 'Round one, Fembly Hussy and Membly Fuzzy. Partners in crime. Destroyers of the constitutional right of the majority. Annihilators of the sacredness of the membly without which no life is possible. Begin.'

Into the ring stepped two little people wearing striped body stockings, each carrying a long pole with tinkling brass bells. The two femblies in the gathering let out long sighs and all the members turned and stared at them with such mournful expressions that the femblies completely covered their eyes and were totally silenced.

The membly who had made the announcement and who was known, Alice later discovered, as the deaferee, called out again, 'Begin.'

One of the creatures backed into a corner and began to sob bitterly. 'I don't want to begin,' it said. 'I want to go home.'

'There, there,' the other said. 'You can go home if you want to. Let's make up again.'

'Bedoing,' went the brass gong. 'Round one to Membly Fuzzy. Two tickets to the football final on Saturday.' The membly looked distinctly pleased. With that the fembly rushed out with her stick and bells and hit him on the top of the head, making an entrancingly musical sound as she did so.

'Oooooh.' The membly gathering groaned and the pyramid hats wobbled precariously. 'Foul,' shouted the deaferee. 'Round two to Membly Fuzzy. Two pints of pinnis per day per month.' A glazed look came over the membly's face. The fembly tore out from her corner and hit him again with the brass bells which this time sounded like a chorus of singing birds. The sound filled the clearing and the two femblies in the gathering covered their ears with their hands and began to rock. One of the pyramid-hatted heads leaned over and tapped them reprovingly on their shoulders. The tap seemed to shrivel them up because to Alice's amazement their grey garments folded in on them as if there were no bodies there at all. But she thought she could see the bright beaming eyes somewhere in the folds of the material. The membly in the ring began to grow bigger. He stuck his chest out and he said, 'You're getting uppity.' The gathering roared with approval and beat the ground with their sticks and feet and bashed their heads and hats off each other. They looked so ridiculous that Alice longed to laugh out loud but she stifled her mirth for fear of being discovered. The fembly in the ring looked amazed at the membly's remark.

'Uppity?' she squeaked. 'Uppity? I never heard of such a thing.'

'Bedoing,' went the deaferee's gong. 'Round three to Membly Fuzzy. Two questions in a row, one denial.'

There were strange rules to this Boxing Match, Alice thought. It looked as if the odds were in favour of the membly. If that were the case what was the point in the exercise? And where were the matches? And who was to be matched? It occurred to her that perhaps it was a mismatch. It was some kind of contest for a mismatch. But who would win? And what would the prize be?

At this point the fembly seemed to become calmer. She appeared to be thinking. Then she dropped onto her little round belly and crawled into the centre of the ring.

'I pray justice,' she said. 'In the name of the great and good I pray justice.'

There was a deadly silence then and the deaferee looked to the gathering for guidance. A few of the pyramid hats shuffled some papers and began to leaf through pages with intense concentration. One of them signalled to the deaferee who descended to consult with him. There was much nodding and shaking of heads and finally the deaferee came back to the ring and called out: 'Round four to Membly Fuzzy. Inappropriate appeal.'

Membly Fuzzy looked worried, but in spite of his worried look he was beginning to swell. By contrast, the fembly was shrinking much in the way that the two femblies in the gathering had shrunk, only her shrinkage was totally visible because of her striped body stocking which now hung loosely around her, the feet trailing like a tail as she crawled back to her corner.

Alice could not contain herself any longer. She leaped to her feet and cried out, 'Where is your justice, you stupid people? Why are you shrinking the femblies? If they shrink any more there will be nothing left.'

She expected an angry response but all she got were some strange stares and more shuffling of paper and a few sniggers from the back rows. The most senior-looking membly stood up, took off his pyramid hat and intoned in a deep voice, 'That is the general id-ee-aa. The shrinkage of the femblies in the boxing ring is the ultimate and only good in itself. It is therefore not moral to decide the fate of either being. All has been pre-ordained. It is in the nature of things that femblies shrink and memblies swell. So it has always been and so it shall always be.'

A great peal of thunder followed his words, the sky darkened and huge drops of rain began to spill on top of everyone.

'Rounds five and six to Membly Fuzzy,' shouted the deaferee above the thunder peals. 'Rain stopped play. Drag away the body.'

There was not much left to drag away. The poor little fembly body stocking seemed completely empty and the poor membly was so swollen and stuffed up he could scarcely walk. He rolled over on his side and began to groan. The deaferee leaned over and took his stick with the bells on it and laid it beside the fembly's stick, which had suddenly sprouted little flowerheads. Out of one of the flowerheads poked a tiny nose and a bright pair of eyes.

'Mamba, famba', called a plaintive voice. The membly rolled off the ring and down the hill and the deaferee followed him, collecting raindrops as he went.

'Mamba, famba,' called the creature. But no one was listening. Alice climbed into the ring and picked it up.

'Mamba, famba, famba, mamba,' cried the creature again and again.

'That's all I need,' said Alice disapprovingly. 'I suppose you'll have to come along with me.' She slipped the creature into her pocket and followed everyone else out of the clearing.

Maeve Kelly

The Twelve Dancing Princesses

The blood tree sheds
its rubies, its molten golds,
groans when his blind weight
snaps a branch
As I go down the slow
spirals his foot treads
on my heels; step by step
he withholds me. Even the ferry
is stern down under
his great cloak. We may not
reach the island.

I cannot drowse him
into heedlessness. Old voices
in the wildwood warn him
of my spiced cup.

How his crotch sags, rogue
bull, old soldier; he
and my father are in league
He has a kingdom to inherit,
and will dog me
until my slippers are spotless,
until my nights dance no longer.

Roz Cowman

Snow-Fight Defeats Patri Arky

SNOW-FIGHT lived with her cousins the Arky family. She had been living there since her mother had died many years before. Though she had been called Snow-White at birth she preferred the name Snow-Fight, which her cousin Patri had begun to call her soon after her arrival, due to their constant arguments about sharing housework.

Snow-Fight had large green eyes and curly red hair, and her skin was so fair that her nine freckles looked as if they had been painted on. She had tried to get along with her cousins, but every day seemed to bring more disagreement and unhappiness.

'Where's my clean shirt?' Patri Arky asked, as he impatiently pulled all the neatly-folded clothes out of the hot press.

'When did you wash it?' retorted Snow-Fight.

'I!' exclaimed Patri, 'When did *I* wash it? Since when did a hard-working man like myself find time to do silly washing?'

'Well,' said Snow-Fight, 'clean shirts don't just appear, you know.'

'Hummph,' muttered Patri, 'I didn't ask for a treatise on the subject, I only want what is due to me.'

'Due? Due?' repeated Snow-Fight incredulously, 'No-one is *due* a clean shirt, you know where the washing machine and the iron are kept if it's a clean shirt you want.'

And so went another prelude to an argument in the Arky household on the politics of housework.

There were seven Arkys, five brothers and two sisters. Ann Arky had left home years before; she could not bear the way her brothers wanted everything organized to suit themselves, expecting herself and her older sister Matri to do simply everything around the house.

The eldest Arky was called Olig. He was haughty and selfish. He insisted on taking the seat at the top of the table at meal times, the seat which was nearest the stove, caring only about his own warmth and comfort. He demanded his dinner first, and if he didn't get it, would sulk and make the meal miserable for everyone else.

Sometimes he had to shove Hier out of his place. Hier Arky was not quite as strong as Olig, but he admired the way his big brother got what he wanted all the time. He also bullied Matri as much as he could, and insisting on having his bed made and his potatoes mashed for him.

Next in age were the twins Mon and Noh Arky. Though twins, they were not alike: Mon (or Monty as he liked to be called) was fascinated by anything regal and he spent his days dreaming about ermine coats, thrones and palaces. He tried hard to order others around as if he were some kind of king!

Noh was a lovely lad, black-haired and gentle. He disliked fighting and never argued with his brothers but he wished he was old enough to go off on an adventure, just like his big sister Ann Arky.

Of all the boys, the one who disliked Snow-Fight most of all was Patri. He had been happy until she had turned up and though he had tried to turn Matri against Snow-Fight and stop her listening to the crazy notions of her cousin, he had failed. Patri had tried to bully Snow-Fight when she first arrived but with her red-haired temper and quick tongue he was no match for her. The only one Snow-Fight felt close to was Matri; she was quiet but strong and always intervened if the boys were giving Snow-Fight a hard time, which they often did. They had become good friends and had great fun together, spending hours talking. Their favourite activity was going on picnics. They loved to walk from the Arky house deep into the woods, where they had discovered a path that led down to the sea-shore. A shared passion was collecting shells and feathers. They were amazed at the colours and shapes of the shells and they tickled each other with the silky feathers. It was always a treat to go out together.

Snow-Fight noticed how increasingly hard Matri was working in the house.

'I worry that you will exhaust yourself, Matri', said Snow-Fight one day as they strolled along through the woods watching the squirrels collect walnuts.

'Oh Snow,' replied Matri, 'You are always worrying about me. Don't fret yourself.'

Snow-Fight nodded slowly, wishing that Matri had fewer demands on her time and didn't have to be constantly reminding her brothers of basic things which Snow-Fight felt everyone should know.

None of the boys picked up their dirty clothes. The younger ones had learned the habits of the older boys, especially Olig and Patri who were so jealous of Snow-Fight that they did things on purpose just to annoy her. Like the way they never put down the toilet seat before leaving the bathroom or they never had time to do the washing. The one occasion Olig did, he put everything in at once and shrank all the clothes.

Since their cousin Snow-Fight had come to live with them, Matri was spending more time in the woods and at the sea than she did in the house. Oftentimes of late the boys had come home to find that their dinner was not ready. Things got even worse for the Arky boys. A dreadful thing occurred one Friday night: they arrived home to find a note on the fridge which said 'Gone to an assertiveness training class', signed Matri.

Several weeks later Matri announced that Snow-Fight and herself were going to a dance and that none of the boys could go, as it was for women and girls only. This was the last straw. Patri decided that something would have to be done.

He thought up a clever plan, one which would ensure

that Matri would stay in the house and which would also take care of that troublemaker Snow-Fight.

Late on the night of the dance Snow-Fight and Matri arrived home. They were laughing and singing songs about women's armies and becoming engineers. Patri was about to tell them to be quiet when he heard other singing voices. With Snow-Fight and Matri were the three Fury sisters. They were bright energetic young women, and had been the organizers of the dance. The five women were swearing loudly that they would all organize another such evening very soon. As they left they sang 'I will survive' in harmony.

Above them in his dark bedroom Patri heard this, and he vowed that if the house was going to be filled with cackling women in this manner on a regular basis, the sooner he carried out his plan the better.

Next day, Snow-Fight woke early and went out to the woods for her morning jog. She did her warm-ups and set off down the worn path towards the sea. There by a large oak was an old man, with a basket of ripe red apples.

'Have a pretty apple, my dear,' said the crackly voice.

'Apples! — you've got to be joking!' puffed Snow-Fight. 'They're either pumped full of chemicals or else irradiated to make them stay fresh, no thanks.' She called back over her shoulder, 'I haven't eaten apples for years.' And she jogged off down the path to the strand.

The disguised Patri sat bewildered; his clever plan had not worked. He *had* to get Snow-Fight somehow. None of the old tricks would work on her. He decided to enlist the help of his old school buddies, the Crats.

The Crats lived two miles away and Patri remembered how they had always been such allies at school. He knew he could depend on their help when they heard how Snow-Fight was disrupting his household.

Otto and Techno Crat listened carefully to Patri. Otto never allowed anyone inside his house, so Patri was given a lecture on how to remain boss in your own home. It was not to Otto Crat that Patri applied for practical assistance, but to

Techno.

Techno Crat brought Patri into his laboratory and here Patri saw all sorts of wonders that Techno was developing. There were gigantic rats and miniscule elephants and little puppies with no tails.

'These', laughed Techno, 'are my pets, they help me greatly with my work as you can see,' and he pointed to rows of cages which lined the walls of his laboratory.

Patri smiled nervously and reminded Techno of his problem. From a long line of test-tubes Techno chose a white liquid which he poured into a tiny phial.

'Put this into her tea and she won't make a sound for years,' snorted Techno. Patri laughed with him as he slipped the thin phial into his pocket and set off for home.

Snow-Fight didn't drink tea or coffee but Patri knew how much she loved a glass of soya milk before her jog. So when he got home and no-one was looking he poured the contents of the phial into her soya milk flask. He didn't have long to wait. That evening as Noh and Mon were walking through the woods they found Snow-Fight stretched out on the path. Tearfully they carried her home and with Olig's help they laid her on the bed. Herface was cold as ice and her breath was barely there, yet Matri saw that she was asleep. It puzzled her to know how Snow-Fight, her beautiful friend, had collapsed into this deep sleep.

Patri hugged himself with glee, thrilled that Snow-Fight was at last silent and that Matri would now be obliged to stay put. He had sorted it all out!

'Soon things will be back to the way they were before Snow-Fight arrived', he whispered to himself as he settled down for the night.

For three days his plan worked beautifully. Matri threw herself into housework, stopping only to check on Snow-Fight. But there was no change in her condition. She slept silently, growing paler each day. On the fourth day there was a loud knock and into the kitchen stumbled the three Fury sisters.

'Oh Matri, how awful, we've just heard about Snow-Fight,' and the three women put their arms around Matri as she burst into tears and wept.

In no time the three Furys had organized things. They took turns sitting with Snow-Fight and they stroked her and spoke to her, even sang, in an effort to waken her. By the time Patri got home his plan had fallen apart. The Furys had decided they would move in and devote their time to Snow-Fight. Matri was, of course, glad of their offer and loved their company. Soon the house was full of their singing and humming. They only visited the kitchen to make soup for Matri or herbal tea for themselves. There were some grumblings from the younger Arky boys but when they realised that no cooking or housework would be done while Snow-Fight was ill, they got stuck in themselves. All, that is, except Patri Arky. He sat slumped on the sofa listening to the crooning and cackling of the women.

'I can't stand this,' he said as he buried his face in his hands, and though he hated to admit defeat he knew that events had taken such a turn against him that things would never be the same again. So he packed a bag and as the clock struck eleven he slipped out of the little house on the edge of the woods and decided to go to find a place where he would receive the respect and attention that he was due.

'Somewhere that those horrid ideas of Snow-Fight's haven't been heard of,' he thought hopefully. 'Ah, for the good old days,' he sighed, as he put distance between himself and the little house.

Patri Arky could not have been gone more than an hour when the front door flew open and in marched Ann Arky, a tall woman with long chestnut-coloured hair and a broad smile on her face. She bounded up the stairs to Snow-Fight's room and the women within shrieked with joy at the sight of their long-lost sister and friend.

Ann Arky had had such adventures. She was now a world-famous scientist and had discovered excellent things like cures for diseases and natural remedies that had long been forgotten. None of her knowledge came from harming animals; she had collected the wisdom of all the wise healers she had found on her travels and she knew just what Snow-Fight needed.

From beneath her purple shawl she pulled a small glass bottle. In it was a mixture of herbs and mosses. She instructed the other women as she placed a drop of this potion on Snow-Fight's eyes and lips. Each of the women kissed Snow-Fight in turn and they all held hands and sang an ancient rhyme which Ann Arky taught them.

WOMEN ARE WE, SISTERS ARE WE,
WE HAVE THE POWER TO HEAL OURSELVES,
WE KILL NO BEASTS, WE POISON NO LANDS,
THE POWER IS OURS, IT IS IN OUR HANDS.

As the last note was sung a sweet perfume filled the room, Snow-Fight opened her eyes and the six women laughed and cheered with relief and happiness.

By the next morning the six women had decided that they would live together, with and for each other. The boys Olig, Mon, Hier and Noh finally agreed that they would build a house further into the wood and that they would visit their sisters. Before they left each of them promised that they would never expect any woman to clean and cook for them. In fact, Noh and Mon were signing up for the cordon bleu cookery class in the local school next term. Snow-Fight believed that now Patri Arky was gone the boys would indeed try to keep their promise.

None of these women thought that they would live happily ever after, as the story goes, but they knew that they would live equally, and what could be nicer?

Grainne Healy

A Tale To Remember

THERE was once a young princess, who was full of energy in mind and body. She spent many hours roaming the fields and hills, gaining knowledge and delighting in the plants and animals. Her parents encouraged her in these pursuits, for they had a deep love of wisdom and wished their daughter to develop herself fully.

When the princess was grown, straight as a young ash plant, it was deemed time for a more formal education, and the parents sent their daughter to the university to study. Indeed, all young people in their kingdom had a full education, for the king and queen believed this to be a wise course that would bring peace and contentment to their land. Their subjects were not so enlightened; they put more value on wealth and status, and although they thought it 'nice' that daughters should study, it was more important to them that they should marry well.

The princess, however, was not bothered by these considerations; she was eager to learn, and took to her studies with pleasure, choosing to study the natural sciences. She worked hard and excelled in all she undertook, and it soon became obvious to her professors and her classmates that she possessed an original and brilliant mind. Even if they envied her they could not dislike her, for she also had a sense of humour, and was not at all conceited.

A certain prince from another kingdom was attending the same university as the princess. He too was highly intelligent, and it so happened that he worked alongside the princess, sharing the same interests as she did. They would sometimes work together and exchange ideas, they would walk in the country looking for rare plants and sit up into the early hours reading aloud to each other. All their friends could see what was happening, but they were unaware of the spell that was overtaking them.

On the day of their graduation the princess was singled out as the one student who had ever, in the whole history of the university, received the highest marks in her studies. The young prince also had excellent results, but none exceeded the princess. The next day, to celebrate their success, the young pair went out walking in their favourite valley. The flowers of the summer were in bloom, birdsong laced the air, bees hummed in the full blossoms; when they bent down to part the grass the better to see a wild orchid, their hands touched, their eyes met in a way they never had before, their bodies were drawn each to each. The love magic was on them both.

So it was that with the blessings of both their families the two young people were married. They both worked hard side by side at their chosen careers, they taught, they wrote, they published their findings, but it was the princess's work that was the most original and exciting. They were as happy as the day was long.

During these first years of married life the princess's learning and wisdom was sought out by scholars from near and far. Her lectures were always fully attended, her publications eagerly awaited. She was held in deep respect in the farthest corners of the kingdom. Then a change came upon her; she published less and less, she refused offers to lecture, those who knew her remarked that her eyes that had been so bright with active intelligence were now dull, that her full laugh was becoming a titter. There were mutterings that she was under some enchantment.

Her husband continued to develop his work, while she did less and less. Often she would ask him to lecture in her stead, while she did things around the house, and as she refused her opportunities, people began to seek the prince out more frequently, so his career prospered and the princess's work declined. The enchantment was so deep upon her that a visiting professor remarked, when he met her, that he was amazed that such a flipperty-gibbet could have produced such original work in the past. He thought perhaps she had burnt-out young.

Now in this life of joys and sorrows there came a time when the prince fell into a sickness. This was no enchantment; the doctors came and pronounced that it was an illness of the nerves and that, unfortunately, they could do very little. The prince's fine mind could no longer function and he sat all day staring at the clouds and saying not a word. The people of the kingdom were sorry for the prince, and even sorrier for his silly young wife, for that is what she had become.

There lived in the kingdom an editor of a learned journal, who had published articles by the prince on a regular basis. He heard of the affliction that the prince suffered and was filled with amazement when articles written by the prince continued to arrive on his desk. He determined to find out the explanation, so he left his home and travelled across the land to visit the prince.

When the editor arrived at the home of the prince and princess he was greeted by a lively woman. Was this the princess who had lost her wisdom, he wondered? The princess welcomed him, and she took him to her husband, who was a sorry sight, vacant, the mind having left him altogether. The editor conversed with the princess, whose wit and vitality charmed him. After much questioning on his part, she admitted that it was she who was writing the articles in her husband's name. Having now solved the mystery, the editor departed, marvelling that the princess was restored and using her gifts to help her husband.

It was a cause of great rejoicing to the princess that in time her husband was cured, he fully regained his fine mind and the health of his body. The enchantment on the princess having lifted to some extent, it would seem that she could now return in full force to her work again, but this was not to be. For as with each week the prince gained health and took to his studies again, so the princess laid down her pen, turned off her word-processor, she stopped reading, she stopped writing. She giggled, she idled away the hours, the days, the weeks, would it become years? Now, freed from her self-imposed task of rescuing her husband, was she not ready to work again and develop her studies further? The evil enchantment returned as if with renewed vigour.

The queen was distracted to see the princess wasting her talents, she begged her to return to the studies that once gave her so much satisfaction, but her pleadings were of no avail. The princess would not heed her; she laughed with her new irritating titter, told her husband and her mother that she would work again, sometime, when she had more time, when she felt like it, and on her desk she placed an elaborate flower-arrangement.

No-one in all the kingdom knew where this evil enchantment came from. Some said it had grown from within herself. Others said it was unnatural for a princess to be so exceptional; others, like her wise mother, tried to encourage her to take up her work again. Nothing made any difference. The princess had become a 'flipperty-gibbet', and the magic held her in its power.

Now, my sisters, listen to this story that I tell, for in every story lies a truth, and this story holds truth in it I'm telling you. For I heard it from the mouth of a wise woman and poet too, who knew this very princess, and had seen her with her own eyes, and heard her wisdom, and then her foolishness. We must remember this tale and be on our guard, for there lie in this world enchantments, within and without, who knows where? They are at their most powerful when we think them dead, or banished from our kingdom never to return. We must be watchful for ourselves and for our daughters, that sly enchantments don't take away our light.

Anne Le Marquand Hartigan

The Budgeen

ONCE upon a time a long time ago there was a country whose customs were very different from ours. For a start everyone wore veils, men and women, so that none of their faces could be seen, and they were very frightened. They did not know what they were frightened of, because it was not the custom to ask. And they were very happy at being afraid. They would spend a lot of time chattering to one another, about how frightened they were and how everyone was afraid: 'God love her', they would say, 'she wouldn't say *boo* to a goose'. And the highest praise was, 'She's frightened of her own shadow'. And, of the men, who were always silent and would stand together at the street-corners looking like clumps of faded nettles, the women as they passed would simper coyly, 'The cat's got their tongues', and would giggle. From morning till night these women tittered, sipped, and skipped.

Except for one little girl called Macha, and she was too busy thinking about why was she supposed to be frightened and what was she supposed to be frightened of. Why could she not see anyone's face, and why could no-one see *her* face? What was the secret? One day, straight out without fear, she said to her father: 'Why is your face covered? I want to see your face.' Her father seized her and began beating her without giving her an answer. She fought back and her hand grabbed hold of his veil and all of a sudden it came away from his face. What was worse, his nose fell off. And there he stood, without a nose.

Her mother cried out, 'What are we going to do? You have ruined us! Your sisters and I will die of shame!' And, as was only proper, they did.

The father, who looked very funny indeed without a nose, and could only speak in muffled croaks, tried to shout: 'Hussy! Are you too not going to die of shame?' But all Macha could do was burst out laughing. He took hold of his sword and went for her: 'Any woman who finds out how easily a man's nose comes off has learned the Secret of the Land and she must die!' And at that he lunged with his sword at her heart, but she was too quick. He fell over his tangled veils which were all about his feet.

Macha ran out of the house and through the streets, shouting, *'Ní scéal rúin é ó tá a fhios ag triúr é!'*, which meant, 'it is not a secret if it is known to three people.' But all the doors and windows were shut and all the people put their fingers in their ears, so there were still only two to know the Secret, as she ran faster and faster like the wind down the bohereens, over the bogs, and deep into the forest where no-one had ventured ever before. There she found a little hut. She could barely make out the words to the humming noise that came from inside:

'Pull a cake, roll a cake,
Budgeen and thumb,
I'll bake you a cake
As quick as they come . . .'

She stood on the window-sill and peered in. There was an old woman inside: she wore no veil. Even though Macha coughed and tapped at the pane, the old woman was too busy kneading dough, pulling it and rolling it, to notice. She was red in the face with her work, putting pieces of rolled dough into the oven and taking other pieces out. What Macha saw so astonished her that she fell right in through the window. There were noses, hundreds and hundreds of noses, all different sizes and shapes. The old woman would take a bit of paper out of her pocket, examine it, check the list against the number of noses in front of her, sometimes fly into a temper, hurl some noses to the floor, stamp on them, and put the dough back into the basin and begin the kneading all over again.

Macha's heart began to beat very fast. She forgot her manners and burst out, 'Who told you the Secret? And who told you to make the noses?' The old woman spun around, roaring with laughter, whirling faster and faster until Macha thought she would disappear altogether. 'Bless me, bless me, the ignorance of this young one! We don't call them noses, we call them budgeens. Men cannot live unless they have their budgeens. I make all the budgeens, I am the *budgeen-maker!*'

Macha faced her: and for the first time in her life she felt fear: 'Why do you keep it a secret and frighten us all?' At this, the old woman stopped her spinning, came firmly down upon two feet, fixed Macha with two eyes like steel. She barked: 'I keep nothing secret! You are keeping a secret from me. Tell it!' Macha said, 'I can't tell it. Because *ní scéal rúin é ó tá a fhios ag triúr é.*' The old woman pursed her lips with annoyance: '*Is olc an chearc nach scríobann di féin:* it's a bad hen that does not scratch for herself! I've been too busy, keeping the breath inside the men, to scratch around and know what's going on behind my back! That robber of a king, that gombeen, that grabber, not letting the women know that men's budgeens fall off! And that I am the one who puts them back on! So that's his power! He sells my new budgeens and tells all the men that *he* makes them, gripping all the praise for himself, and keeping it a secret too! No more, no more, he can fool some of the people all of the time and all of the people some of the time but he won't fool old Morrígan more than once! I'm going on strike, I'm retiring. Let *you* take your turn at keeping the world going.'

And thereupon she blew out her fire, dismantled her oven, put it in her pocket, poured water on all the dough, and threw it out of the hut so ferociously that all the animals, birds, trees and plants of the forest began to screech in chorus, 'Tell it to a third,' they screamed, 'tell it to a third, Macha, tell it to a third!' Old Morrígan got hold of her bellows and began puffing the air between Macha's feet so vigorously that the girl lost her balance and floated up into the air, out of the window, and over the trees. As she went, she heard Morrígan's voice like a thin pipe following her: 'You have already one gift, the gift of fearlessness: I give you two more — the gift of speed and the gift of the budgeen-recipe.'

Macha's veil was like a sail: it carried her over mountains, rivers, and lakes, like a white mare flying, then a grey one, then a black one. At nightfall she alighted at a small farm-house. Inside there was a man asleep. By his posture he seemed a very wretched unhappy man. She took the veil off his face and never had she seen such a miserable budgeen in all her life, all cracked and soggy.

She went to the cupboard, got a bowl, fresh flour and water, lit the oven; and in a few minutes had baked him a fine brown shiny new one, and stroked it into place. The man (whose name was Crunnchu) woke up dancing with joy. 'I'm a new man, I've no need to go to the king any more, I have *you!* Are we not the best match?' 'We are,' she said, 'but never tell the king!'

So for a while they lived happily together, until one day a message came from the king that there was a great curse upon the land and all the men had to come to his council. Crunnchu went. Late that night he returned and said, 'Oh what have I done? I've let the cat out of the bag. The king told us the land is cursed because there are no new noses: and *I* was fool enough to tell *him* that Macha is a budgeen-maker and she can lift the curse. The king said, "bring her to me": and I knew from the way he winked that once he has got your recipe from you he will kill you.' Macha smiled to herself, because she still had one gift the king knew nothing of. 'Go back to the king, and tell him I will be glad to meet with him: on one condition. It must be tomorrow, the day of the horse-races, and the king's horse must race against me.' Crunnchu implored her not to be so reckless, how could a woman run faster than a horse? She repeated her command, and he did her bidding.

The king thought it a great joke. But Macha stayed up all

night, baking.

The next day she arrived at the assembly with a bag of new budgeens strapped to her back. The horn sounded, the race commenced. Her gift of speed from Morrígan brought her to the winning-post in one leap: she faced the king as he galloped toward her. She opened her mouth, and it grew and grew, wider and wider. The wider the mouth grew, the more the men froze with fear. Then she swallowed the king, right out of his saddle.

She hitched up her skirts and began a jig, kicking her legs higher and higher; the women threw off their veils, hitched up *their* skirts too, and *their* legs likewise were joining in the jig. All that could be seen were the legs up and down in the air and the noise was like a hundred thunderstorms: the birds joined in and the fishes from the sea, and all the creatures of the land, and even the sun and the moon.

The women picked up the cry, 'Tell it to a third, tell it to a third!' As she danced, Macha gave a great gulp of breath, and out shot the king into the crowd from between her thighs. He fell to the ground in one place; and his budgeen fell in another, crumbling into dust.

She said, 'There's a new one for you in the sack on my back.' How the women laughed to see him crawl to put it on!

'If men steal women's work,' she said, 'and claim it for their own, I will not just swallow *one*, but the *lot* of you!' And the men never dared pull such a stroke ever again.

Margaretta D'Arcy

Ms Snow White Wins Case In High Court

In a landmark decision handed down in Court yesterday by Ms Justice Goodbye, Snow White was granted an injunction against seven men. MARK MIWORD reports on the case.

SNOW WHITE was yesterday granted an injunction in the High Court in Dublin, restraining a total of seven men from entering on or interfering with the premises in the heart of the woods, which had been shared between them for ten years. The Court heard how Ms White had been abused for a total of ten years by the defendants, since she was seven years old. In an *ex tempore* judgement, Ms Justice Goodbye said that it was the worst case she had ever been forced to hear.

At the conclusion of the hearing, which lasted four days, there was uproar from the seven defendants, who had to be carried forcibly from the body of the Court. Gardai were forced to arrest three of the defendants as they emerged, and all pleaded guilty to a breach of the peace in a special sitting of the District Court, and were fined £2 each and bound over.

Yesterday was devoted entirely to the judgement, as evidence had been taken earlier from both the plaintiff and the defendants. In outlining the evidence which had been given, Justice Goodbye said that it was obvious that the defendants had, by their own admission, never made any attempt to offer retribution to Ms White, and that the worst aspect of the entire case was that they had shown no remorse for their actions over the years. In fact, the contrary was the case, as the defendants sought to justify their behaviour, and thereby compounded the wrong.

Justice Goodbye outlined the circumstances under which the case came before her. Ms White had been abandoned in the heart of the forest, when she was seven years old, by an agent acting on behalf of her stepmother, who wished to get rid of her. She pointed out, inter alia, that it was open to bring an action for cruelty on foot of this. Ms White, after wandering around for some considerable time, had then stumbled on a small house. Exhausted, she had lain down to sleep. Upon awakening, she was confronted by seven men, who were returning home from work as gold-diggers. Justice Goodbye made the point that Ms White was in no fit mental or physical condition, by virtue of her age and circumstances, to make any decision which could amount under any circumstances to mean 'the right to choose', in the legal sense of the word. Consequently, everything which took place following the initial encounter was tainted.

Messrs Dopey, Sneezy, Happy, Grumpy, Doc, Sleepy and Bashful proceeded to enter into a contract with Ms White, who was still exhausted, and in any event, of an age not legally held to be old enough to enter into a contract. Effectively under duress, Ms White agreed — following various promptings from the seven men — to look after the house while they were out gold-digging. She also agreed to cook and wash for all seven, to make all the beds, to sew and knit and generally look after their welfare. Ms Justice Goodbye said that the contract, apart from its earlier mentioned failings, was derelict further in so far as there was no limit to the contractual obligations entered upon by Ms White. In return for agreeing to those conditions, Ms White was allowed to sleep in the house, and also have enough food to eat. The contract was, in the words of Justice Goodbye, 'a travesty of natural justice'. She said also that Ms White must have been 'the handiest slave these seven men would ever have the good fortune to encounter'.

The seven men were so content with their lot that they

took to singing songs upon their exit from the house each morning, and upon their return in the evening. Ms Justice Goodbye outlined the duties which Ms White was expected to perform. She was forced to get up two hours before any of the seven men, and prepare their breakfast. At the same time, she had to gather wood to light the fire and ensure that the house was clean by the time the seven decided it was time for them to get up. She herself did not get anything to eat until they left. On occasion, there was very little food left and she was forced to wait until dinner time before she ate properly.

With regard to the washing of their clothes, Ms Goodbye rehearsed the evidence that had been given to the effect that the seven never took any care of themselves when they were out digging for gold. Knowing that they had someone at home to do 'all the dirty work', their behaviour was such as to suggest that they were deliberately creating work for Snow White. Ms White had given evidence of the filthy nature of all seven men. They left their clothes where they fell before they went to bed, and she was expected to cater to their smallest whim. This, said Justice Goodbye, was somewhat at odds with the claim of the defendants' Counsel that all seven were self-styled New Age men in touch with their own feelings and emotions. Throughout all of this, the seven men continually reminded Snow White that on no account should she attempt to open the door during their absence. To this end, they warned her about all manner of dangers which she might face should she disobey them. Justice Goodbye pointed out that even though this 'warning' might well be grounded in a genuine concern for Ms White's 'welfare', the defendants had brought no evidence forward during the hearing to support their claim. The result of these 'warnings' was that Ms White lived in virtual isolation for many years, unaware that around the cottage a small township, Crumlin, had grown up.

As Ms White reached maturity, it appeared to her that the seven men became more 'friendly', in her own words, and she believed that they were viewing her in a different light from hitherto. Gradually, it became clear that some of the seven had designs on her. Justice Goodbye pointed out that it was left to Ms White herself to make clear that 'conjugal rights' had been no part of the original contract. The Justice took the view that this was 'outlandish behaviour' on the part of some of the seven, and that 'it was an extension of the contract which no right-thinking person' would agree with.

The defendants, said Ms Justice Goodbye, had given evidence to the effect that throughout their careers as gold-diggers, they had made what they described as 'a fair bit of money'. However, none of this wealth had ever found its way to Ms White, nor indeed had gone any way towards making her life in the house any easier. The Justice said that the only conclusion that could be drawn was that the seven had hidden their wealth, and that they had no intention, even at this late stage, of making any amends to Ms White. The Justice also pointed out that it was open to Ms White to enter a claim on the entire property in the woods, with a view to ensuring complete title to the entire estate. The Justice felt that 'any Court in the land would surely look most favourably on any such claim'. Consequently, Justice Goodbye said that she had no hesitation in making an order restraining all seven defendants from entering on or inter-fering with the house in the woods. Leave to appeal was refused.

After the disturbances, during which one of the defendants, Mr Grumpy, started to shout abuse at the Justice, Ms White appeared outside the Court with her close friend and supporter, Ms Rapunzel. Speaking to reporters, Ms White said that her life had been 'like a bad fairytale' for the past ten years.

Last night, a spokesperson for the Irish Council for Civil Liberties said that they wished Ms White 'all the best for the future' but that the judgement itself held 'grimm prospects' for other cases in that every person who thought they had a similar case as Ms White might now take an action, but that the action might fail, and thus 'hopes would be raised which might not be fulfilled'. The Council said that it was exploring the setting up of a Working Party to look at the implications of this case for all gold-diggers. At some time in the future they may, or may not, publish a report.

Clodagh Corcoran

Grainne's Version Of The Pursuit

DAMN. Feck anyway. I got all tied up in that magic of Celtic romance, the tragic love bit, all because Daddy wanted to marry me off to the head buck cat of the Fenians — gee no, I get so confused nowadays, no, no, the Fianna, you know the band of Fine Things prancing about the country on the little feats of great deeds: how many fine things can you balance on the tip of a sally-rod syndrome? Jumping over heaps of stones, shooting their little thingies and terrifying every decent-living rabbit in the woods.

Red Riding Hood?

Ah no, that was just a wolfish lay in the forest ... there must be a word to alliterate with forest? *ffrench? frolic?* ... forget it! Yeah, the lads? Anyway, Daddy, known as Conn of the 100 Bottles, swore right and wrong, black and white, that I should marry this Fionn-thing, but he was as old as a bush, a pot-bellied, paw-marked, bandy-legged old bollox — no dear, it has nothing to do with hydraulics. You see he was a smoked-salmon socialist when he was young, he ate loads of it, he rigged up a little smokery near the Boyne, but lo and behold the salmon had a quare effect on him, and every time he stuck his thumb in his mouth he got into a time-warp, he could see the devil and all back in the future and onto the past, a form of *salmon eile*, it was said. Well, that gave him a great excuse for oral gratification. Now, I wouldn't be into that kind of thing at all. You see, I fancied his sister, she was something else. I tried to get her on my staff at the Palace, as Mistress of the Bath, in an advisory capacity of course, but no go, she had an innate fear of water.

Everything was fine and ticking over nicely until Daddy decided to have a bit of a shamozzle at Tara for the lads. He intended to hand me over to the Fionn-thing with the enlarged thumb the same night. No way was I going to spend the rest of my life with that fish-eating, thumb-sucking, toothless old queen, not at all. Actually, my own lover was in computers, we met at a fun-weekend in Cork, but she couldn't relocate to Tara, and Daddy had a thing about Cork, something about bottles and the ballgame. But Gobnait came up most weekends for a royal fling, she usually brought a load of young hopefuls with her, she was motorized you know, a little medieval gad-about, very economical and perfect for the conditions. It was all getting a bit trying, she there and I here, and what the hell was happening with the young hopefuls between the weekends. I heard rumours of late-night poker-schools and heavy betting. I began to have my doubts. So we tried co-counselling, but really Cork is centuries from Tara, and Gobnait fell in a big way for one of the co-counsellors. What could we do but opt for open-relating — that last refuge of promiscuous passion — sure we might as well have been trying to pick primroses in October. It was open alright, so open that I was tripping over co-counsellors and computer-operators at every turn. Finally, I got myself disentangled, and Gobnait legged it back to Cork with her bevy of budding beauties. We're supposed to be 'friends' according to the best regulated relationships, like getting it together again when things become too boring with the hopefuls. But really, I couldn't stand the pace, and I grew tired of the daily fax from Gobnait which was a lengthy progress report on her various conquests.

However, back to the Fairytale. Fiona, Fionn's sister had this great body, she had a brain too, but she didn't have much up-front — that proved an advantage. She was much younger than Fionn, but she was still within the older woman bracket. I really fell for her at the Fairytale Congress, she looked ravishing in the garb of Gaeldom and she gave one of the keynote addresses on 'Fairies and the Media'. She was absolutely brilliant. All the fairies and the media highly approved of her speech; in fact, I heard a wimp whisper to a co-wimp something about her magic wand. Instead of giving him a kick in that place where he should have had something, I turned cerebral and had a brainwave.

So the night of the shamozzle Fiona arrived as the dashing Diarmuid Ó Duibhne; she looked fantastic in a tuxedo and neither Daddy nor the lads copped a thing.

Well, you know the rest of it. I had become quite fed-up with the Tara thing, I wanted my own space, get away to the country, find some little place near the sea, I thought of Clare, doesn't everyone, and frankly, I've had my exhilarating moments at the Willie Week in Miltown Malbay. No, Clare seemed too hectic, the kind of place bound to be strewn with everyone who was anyone's ex-lover.

Everything was hunky-dory at the shamozzle, the lads got pissed out of their pelts — they tried to blame me for that, of course, they tried to blame me for every damn thing that happened.

Next morning, the Fionn-thing was the first to sober up, the old bollox. He tried to convince everyone that Diarmuid/Fiona was really Aonghus in drag, just in case things weren't confused enough, and he set off hot-foot in pursuit.

Fiona and myself knew all about the Fionn-thing's real passion for young men, he had had his eye on Diarmuid for quite a long time, you know, all this beating about the bush, brideshead and revisiting, it's all one big hunt with them anyway. So we decided to capture the wimp Diarmuid and drag him along with us, hoping to trade him to Fionn for a huge amount of venture capital, seeing as dowry was completely out for us.

If I were to tell you all that happened to us on the way you'd be here until the cows came home, or another Dark Age had descended upon us. We went all over the place, we got stranded once near Portumna, we were trying to make it to Limerick, we heard it was a real buzz place for women's things. Anyway, we got stuck in a bog, but I found a local eejit and promised him joy if he'd carry us across the bog on his back. He fell for it, but needless to say for him there was no joy.

We did the Ring of Kerry and Sliabh Luachra, we nearly fell foul of a group of non-nationals in a medieval bus, but we diverted them to Dingle and told them that if they were lucky they'd catch the tailend of the Fairytale Congress. We headed back into the mountains and while we were there we really felt the presence of Bridget.

We made it to Limerick, but it was all very het', so we moved up the coast as quick as we could. We came to Sligo and liked the scene, it seemed safe enough, there was nothing to disturb us, even the dead and buried poets who drew thousands to the area under bare Ben Bulben's Head were rumoured not to be there at all. Fiona was of the opinion that that was the result of too much academic research; if you kept scratching and scrapping long enough you'd end up with nothing. She began making notes for the next Congress, she would give a paper which would resound through the world of Fairy and throw the reigning witch, who was always delighted to see everyone and indeed a delight herself, off her throne or her broom forever.

The politics of Fairies was all very well, but it was only when we were settled in that Fiona asked if I were a top or a bottom? Then I discovered that she was heavy into S & M. It went with the territory, she informed me, and what the hell did I think she majored in while on scholarship in Ohio if not S & M. Me, poor fool, thought it had something to do with female spirituality.

Damn anyway. Chains are all very well for bulls — but that's another story I'd better leave to Maeve herself. So I decided on the spot that I was celibate. I faxed Fionn and told him to remove his sister and his wimp, Diarmuid. As for the venture capital, I told him to stuff it, and I didn't give a hoot about the live-register or his small-industry programme, just take the whole bloody lot of them back to Tara, and leave me to my nine bean rows and my little honeybee, and if I were very lucky I might persuade some of the orders of vestals who hung about the mouth of the Liffey to come to me on retreat. Fionn said he would put in a good word with one of the brightest of them, a tacky little number who drove her own car and a very hard bargain. She sounded a comfort in small doses. We left it at that. I got into a warm herbal bath and heard the hounds yelping in the further woods, Fionn would have to have his sport. I never really knew what happened to them afterwards, but as I relaxed in the bath, a comely maiden rode up on horseback, lived locally she said, something about being home on holidays from Liverpool or was it Birmingham, her sister was into politics, but she was a feminist.

Rita Kelly